"Many proclaim themselves loyal,
but who can find one worthy of trust?"
—Proverbs 20:6

Visit us on the Web!
rhcbooks.com
BerenstainBears.com

Educators and librarians, for a variety of teaching tools, visit us at RHTeachersLibrarians.com

Library of Congress Control Number: 2021948454
ISBN 978-0-593-30242-2 (trade) — ISBN 978-0-593-30521-8 (ebook)

MANUFACTURED IN CHINA
10 9 8 7 6 5 4 3 2 1

The Berenstain Bears
Gifts of the Spirit
Trust

Mike Berenstain

Based on the characters created by
Stan and Jan Berenstain

Random House 🏠 **New York**

It was time for spring-cleaning in the Bear family's tree house. And where better to start than the attic? If any place ever needed cleaning up, it was the Bear family's attic. It hadn't been given a thorough cleaning in years. It was full of all kinds of the most amazing stuff— things they had quite forgotten about.

There was Uncle Harry's collection of antique coffee grinders and Great-Grandma's trunks full of fancy hats and feather boas. There were stacks of Papa's old rock-and-roll records and piles of Mama's cookbooks. There was a croquet set with a broken mallet and a piece of furniture they couldn't even identify. Maybe it was a hat rack. Everything was covered with dust and cobwebs. It would take hours to clean up.

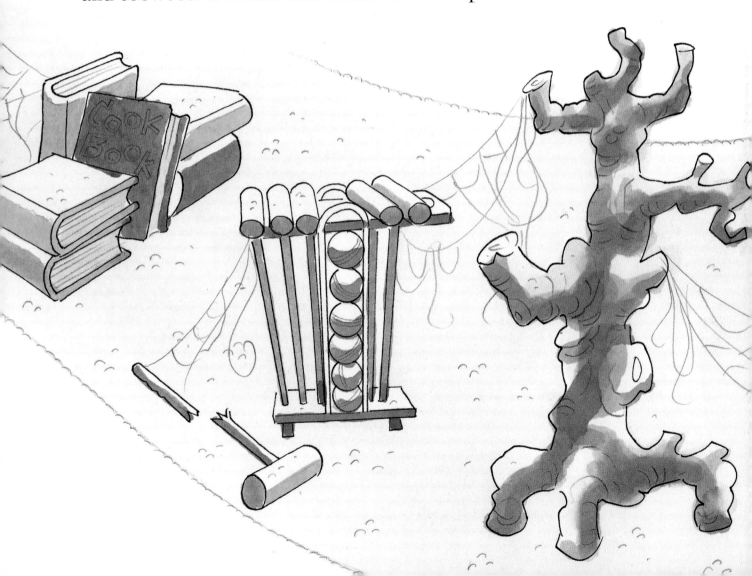

"Can we help in the attic?" asked Brother. All that weird stuff up there looked interesting. Maybe they would find old toys or other fun things.

"We appreciate the offer," said Papa. "But you can help in another way."

"Honey is really too small to help out," Mama explained. "There are too many things for her to get into. It's just not safe."

"You two can keep an eye on Honey downstairs while we work upstairs," said Papa. "Okay?"

"Sure!" agreed Sister. "But when you're done, can we help with the other cleaning?" Maybe they wouldn't get to explore the attic. But messing around with mops and buckets of water would be fun. There might even be a chance for a water fight.

"Of course!" said Papa. "We'll all pitch in."

The cubs settled down in the family room to watch a little TV.
"What'll it be?" asked Sister, turning the channels. "How about *Bearbie's Beach House Adventure*?"

"You've got to be kidding!" said Brother. "I like *Spider-Bear*."

"So do I," replied Sister. "But we've watched it about twenty times."

"It's so good!" said Brother.

"How about *Beary Potter and the Sorcerer's Honey Pot*?" asked Sister. "We both like that."

"Okay!" agreed Brother. "*Beary Potter* it is!"

So they turned on one of their favorites, the story of a brave young wizard and his friends in wizarding school.

Honey watched along with her brother and sister but soon got bored. Nobody had asked her what she wanted to watch, and *Beary Potter* wasn't really her style. Honey liked shows about cute bunnies and happy little ponies.

She started playing with her blocks instead. She was building a playhouse for her bunny and pony toys.

After a while, Honey felt hungry. Maybe it was time for a little snack. She glanced at Brother and Sister. They were involved with their show. It would be a shame to bother them. She'd look for a snack by herself.

Quietly tiptoeing out of the room, she headed for
the pantry. Brother and Sister did not notice.

Before long, Mama and Papa took a break from their attic cleanup and came downstairs to check on the cubs. They found Brother and Sister happily watching TV. But where was Honey?

Quickly, they looked around the house. They looked in the family room—no Honey. They looked in the dining room—no Honey. They looked in the kitchen—no Honey. Then they looked in the pantry.

Inside the pantry, Mama and Papa found lots of honey. Their sweet little Honey Bear was having a snack of her favorite treat— gooey, sticky, yummy *honey*. It was all over her—all over her hands, all over her face, all over her clothes, and all in her fur!

"Brother! Sister!" called Mama and Papa.

Brother and Sister came out of their TV trance. Uh-oh! they thought. Where was Honey? Looking guiltily at each other, they joined Mama and Papa in the pantry.

It was quite a sight — Honey was a gooey, sticky mess!

"Well, what have you two got to say for yourselves?" said Papa. "You were supposed to keep an eye on Honey."

"We were watching TV," confessed Brother.

"I guess we didn't notice what Honey was up to," added Sister, shrugging.

"That's just the point!" said Mama. "You were supposed to pay attention to her. We trusted you to take care of your little sister. What if she had gotten into something dangerous instead of just honey?"

Brother and Sister hung their heads. They realized Mama and Papa were right. They wanted to be trustworthy, and they certainly didn't want their little sister to get into anything dangerous.

"Well, there's something you can do to make up for your mistake," said Mama.

"Really?" said the cubs eagerly. "What is it?"

"You can clean up the honey on our little Honey here!" said Mama. That made Papa laugh. And after a moment, the cubs laughed, too.

But cleaning the honey out of Honey's fur was no laughing matter. It was a tangled, yucky mess!

"One thing's for sure," said Sister as she shampooed
Honey's head in the bathtub. "With all this honey on you,
you definitely are a sweet little thing!"
And that put them all in a good mood once more.